For my friend, Phoebe Gilman.
F. W.

For Gabriel and Apple, with thanks to Dr Hok.
N. L.

JENNIFER JONES WON'T LEAVE ME ALONE
A DOUBLEDAY BOOK 0385 60258 8

Published in Great Britain by Doubleday,
an imprint of Random House Children's Books

This edition published 2003

1 3 5 7 9 10 8 6 4 2

Copyright © Frieda Wishinsky, 2003
Illustrations copyright © Neal Layton, 2003

The right of Frieda Wishinsky and Neal Layton to be identified as the author
and illustrator of this work has been asserted in accordance with the
Copyright, Designs and Patents Act 1988.

All rights reserved. No part of this publication may be reproduced, stored in a
retrieval system, or transmitted in any form or by any means, electronic,
mechanical, photocopying, recording or otherwise, without the prior permis-
sion of the publishers.

RANDOM HOUSE CHILDREN'S BOOKS
61-63 Uxbridge Rd, London W5 5SA
A division of The Random House Group Ltd.

RANDOM HOUSE AUSTRALIA (PTY) LTD
20 Alfred Street, Milsons Point, Sydney,
New South Wales 2061, Australia

RANDOM HOUSE NEW ZEALAND LTD
18 Poland Road, Glenfield, Auckland 10, New Zealand

RANDOM HOUSE (PTY) LTD
Endulini, 5A Jubilee Road, Parktown 2193, South Africa

THE RANDOM HOUSE GROUP Limited Reg. No. 954009
www.kidsatrandomhouse.co.uk

A CIP catalogue record for this book is available from the British Library.

Printed and bound in Singapore

Jennifer Jones
won't Leave Me Alone

Frieda wishinsky

Neal Layton

DOUBLEDAY

Jennifer Jones won't leave me alone.
She sits by my side.
She **SHOUTS** in my ear.

She tells me she loves me.
She calls me her 'dear'.

WELL, WE DON'T aND I HaTE IT!

I've had quite enough.
I wish that she'd move
And take all her stuff.

She could move to the jungle
And live in a tree

And talk to the monkeys,
Instead of to me.

But if she insists
That she's not going there,

She could head for the Arctic
And bother a bear.

Or fly to
the desert

Or go to the moon.

I really don't care,
As long as it's soon.

Hurrah! Hallelujah!

Guess what I just heard?
Jennifer's moving.
Her mum's been transferred.

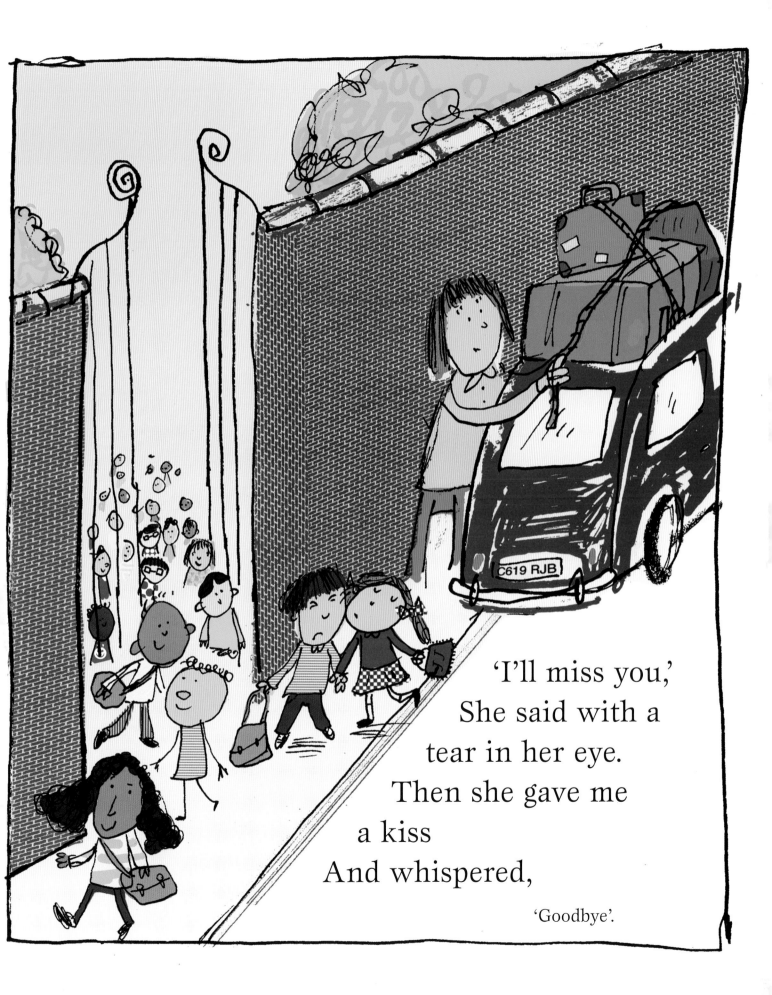

'I'll miss you,'
She said with a
tear in her eye.
Then she gave me
a kiss
And whispered,

'Goodbye'.

Now her seat is all empty.
There's nobody there.
There's no one to kiss me.

There's no one to care.

So I write in my notebook.
I add and subtract.
I study my spelling.
I learn a new fact.

But it's boring! It's lonely!
I miss her a lot.
I wish she'd return

To her usual spot .

And to make matters worse
She writes:

It's divine
Seeing paris at night,

sailing boats down the Rhine,

Munching chocolates in Brussels,

Eating pizza in Rome,

Nibbling viennese pastries you can't get at home.

Oh, she's having such fun,
I thought in despair.

She'll never come home.
She'll stay over there.

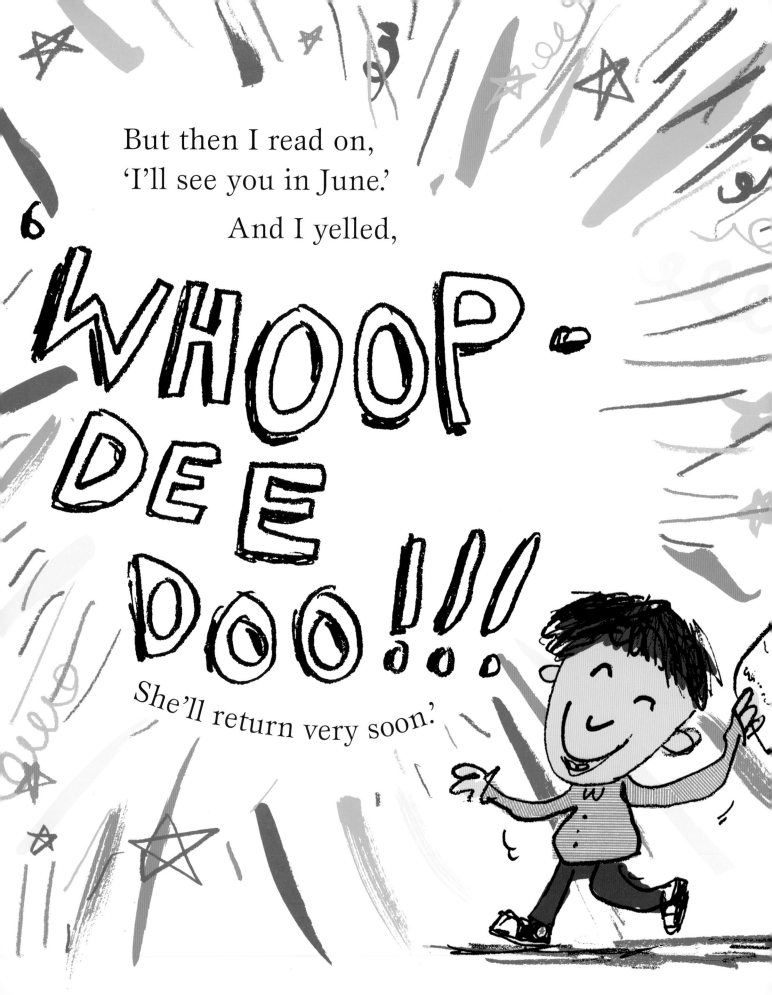

But then I read on,
'I'll see you in June.'
And I yelled,

WHOOP-
DEE
DOO!!!

She'll return very soon.'

6

And as soon as I did,
The kids wondered why
I was jumping and shouting.
So I thought,

But I told them the truth
As I opened the door,
And I ran off to buy

Red hearts at the store